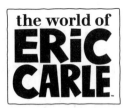

THE VERY BUSY
DOODLE BOOK

A GOLDEN BOOK • NEW YORK

ERIC CARLE™, THE WORLD OF ERIC CARLE™, THE VERY HUNGRY CATERPILLAR™ (name and image).
Illustrations copyright © 2011 Eric Carle LLC. Licensed by Chorion Rights Limited.
The Very Hungry Caterpillar is published by Penguin Group (USA). All rights reserved.
Published in the United States by Golden Books, an imprint of Random House Children's Books, a division of Random
House, Inc., 1745 Broadway, New York, NY 10019, and in Canada by Random House of Canada Limited, Toronto.
Golden Books, A Golden Book, and the G colophon are registered trademarks of Random House, Inc.

ISBN: 978-0-375-87350-8

www.randomhouse.com/kids

Printed in the United States of America

10 9 8 7 6 5 4 3 2 1

To find out more about Eric Carle books and merchandise, visit www.eric-carle.com and
the Eric Carle Museum of Picture Book Art at www.carlemuseum.org.

When you see the Doodlebug, you can say
"Doodlebug! Doodlebug!" out loud
to get your imagination going—and
draw whatever comes to mind!

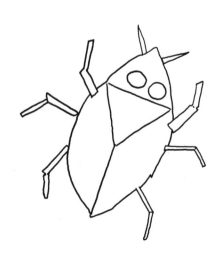

The sun is coming up.
You might like to draw birds chirping at sunrise.

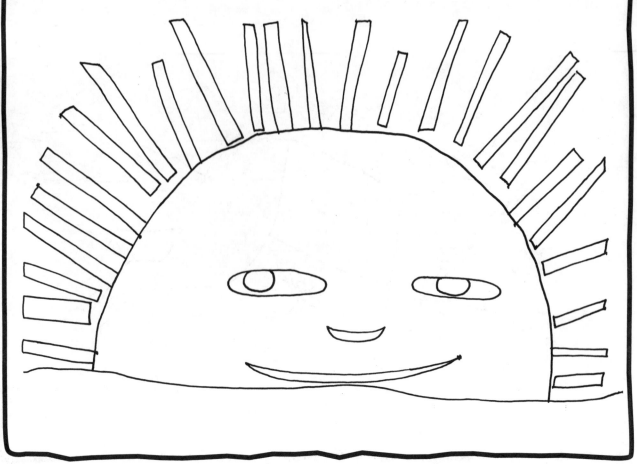

What is the cat chasing? A firefly!
Can you draw a moon and some stars?

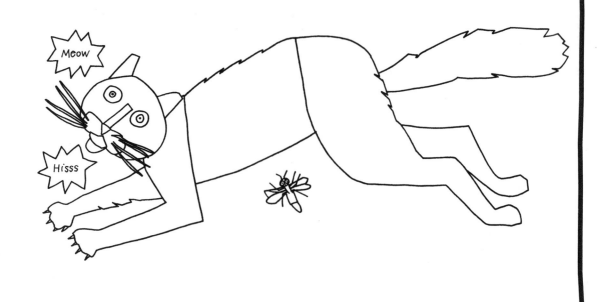

The apple is red.
What else would you like to draw that is red?

You might like to use lots of
colors to decorate these three butterflies.

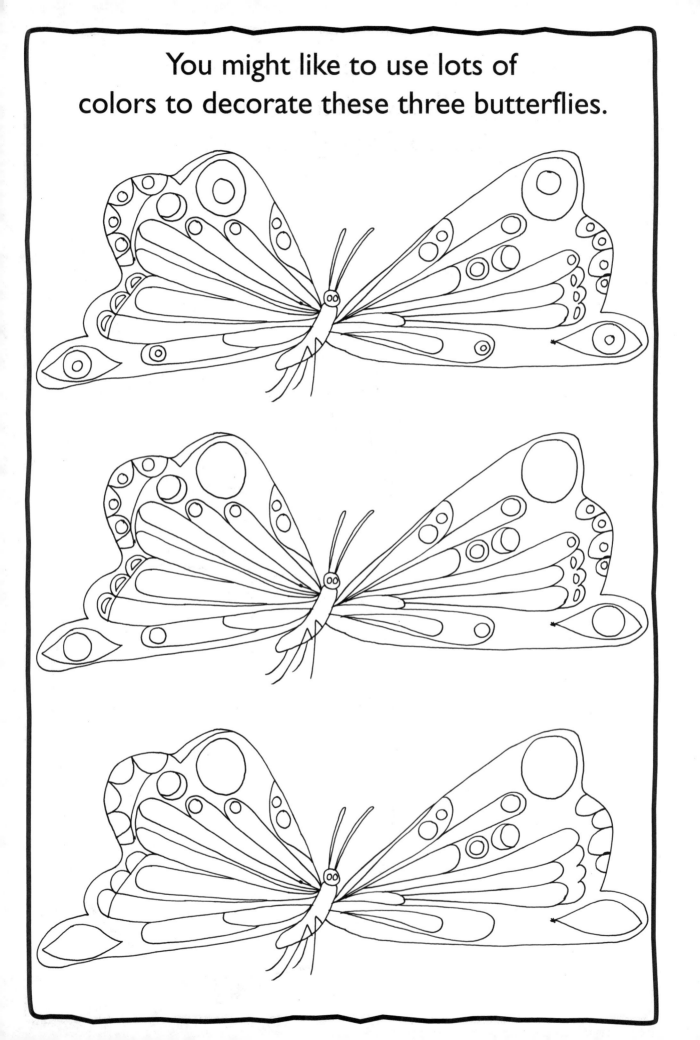

There's a noise outside the window.
See if you can draw what is making the sound.

Can you color the letters in your name?

ABCDEF
GHIJKL
MNOPQ
RSTUV
WXYZ

Can you draw yourself
with these children?

A lollipop can have colorful swirls.
Can you draw your favorite treat?

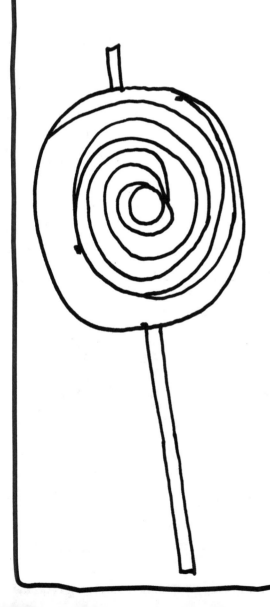

What a sunny day!
Can you draw a picture of yourself doing your favorite activity in the sunshine?

Can you draw an animal living in this shell?

Doodlebug! Doodlebug!

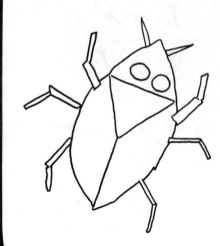

This is a praying mantis.
Try to draw your own insect with
four legs and two spiky arms.

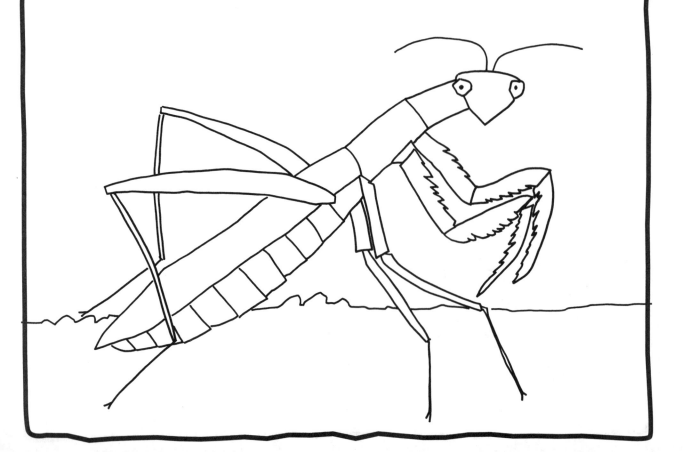

Can you color this slice of watermelon?
What kind of fruit do you like to eat?

Can you finish this skinny caterpillar?
When you're done, draw a picture
of him when he is big and round.

Some cows are black and white. Is there another animal you can draw that is black and white?

Can you complete the
pattern and color the fruit?

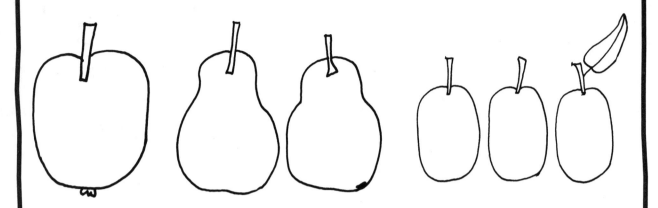

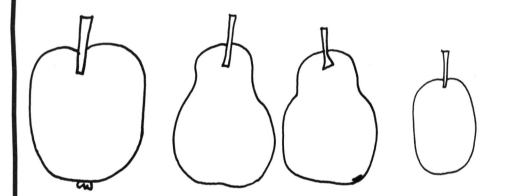

Can you draw a big peacock
tail on this girl's costume?

Try drawing two more dogs,
one big and one small!

How old are you?
Can you color that number?

0123
456
789

What kind of face do you think the sun has?
Can you draw it?

A very hungry caterpillar loves lollipops.
Can you draw two more
lollipops for him to taste?

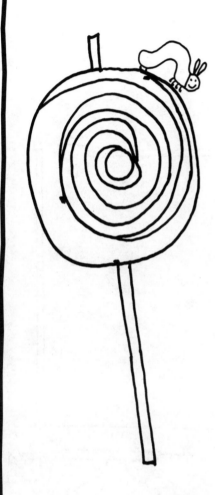

There are two lions in the train car.
Is there another animal with a mane
that you can draw in the train car?

This cheese is yellow.
What else would you
like to draw that is yellow?

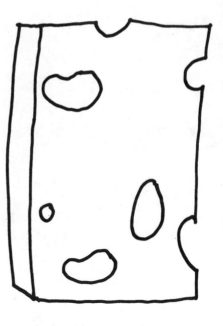

The locust is in a field of flowers.
Can you draw the colorful flowers?

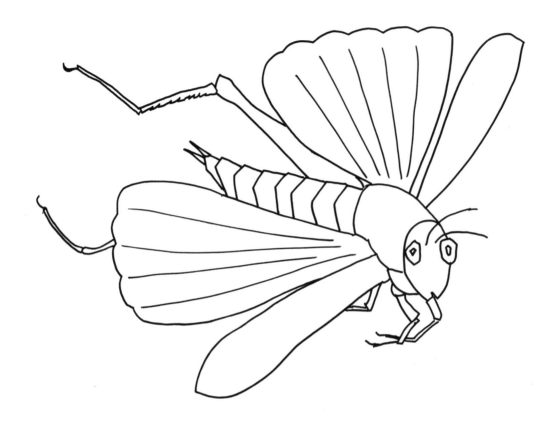

A pickle is green.
What else would you
like to draw that is green?

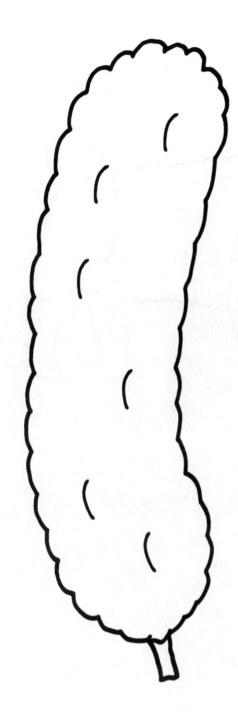

The dog has a new friend!
Would you like to draw
the new friend for him?

Can you decorate the beautiful butterfly wings?

Alligator begins with the letter *A*.
What other animals begin with *A*?
Can you draw one of them?

ALLIGATOR

Can you draw another flying luna moth?

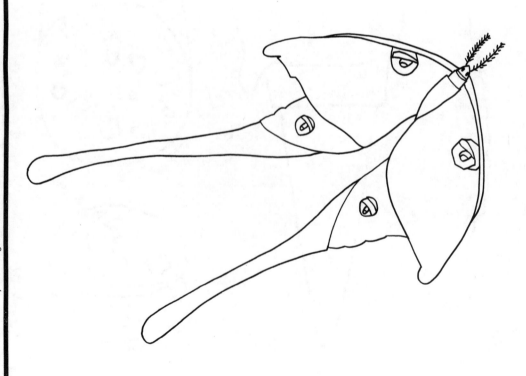

Can you color only the sweet foods?

Doodlebug! Doodlebug!

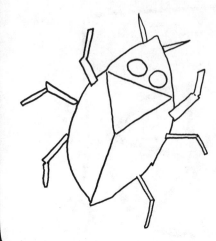

Try to draw as many balloons
as you can for the balloon man to sell.

Can you draw a lily pad
for this frog to sit on?

Can you draw two insect
friends for this quiet cricket?

This leaf is part of a tree.
Can you draw the whole tree?

This worm loves to munch on fruit.
What other kinds of fruit
can you draw for him to eat?

Are you looking in or out the window?
Can you draw what you see?

Can you draw two more sausages
to create a sausage link?
You might also like to add two
eggs for a delicious breakfast!

Can you draw the place where the horse sleeps at night?

Can you draw a flock of sheep in a field?

Bear begins with the letter *B*.
What other animals begin with *B*?
Can you draw one of them?

A very hungry caterpillar
is going to eat four strawberries.
Can you draw three more strawberries?

How many people are in your family?
Can you color that number?

0123

456

789

Can you draw a cozy nest for this duck?

You might enjoy decorating the cupcake!

Can you color the four wings on this dragonfly?

This very hungry caterpillar ate five oranges.
What other fruits do you think he would like?
Can you draw them?

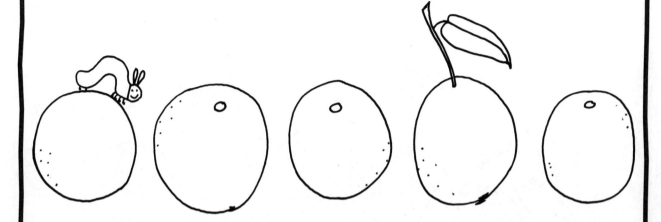

Can you draw a big ball
of yarn for this cat to play with?

Doodlebug! Doodlebug!

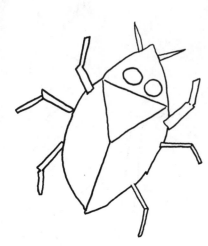

Try to draw some more flowers
for the bumblebee to visit.

The hippo is taking a drink from a river. Can you draw the river?

Can you draw a web like
the one the spider has spun?

An alligator is looking at a pond.
Can you draw the pond, some fish, and anything else you imagine might be in your pond?

Can you draw the tail on the elephant?
Add a big snack for the elephant to eat.

Try to draw the moon and
some more stars for a night scene.

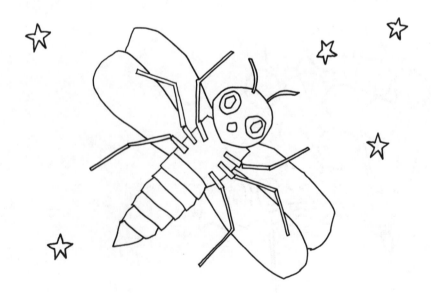

Can you draw people visiting the zoo?

Can you draw some of the animals you might see at the zoo?

This monkey would like to meet you!
Can you draw yourself acting like a monkey?

Can you add two antennae to the locust's head and draw a locust friend for him?

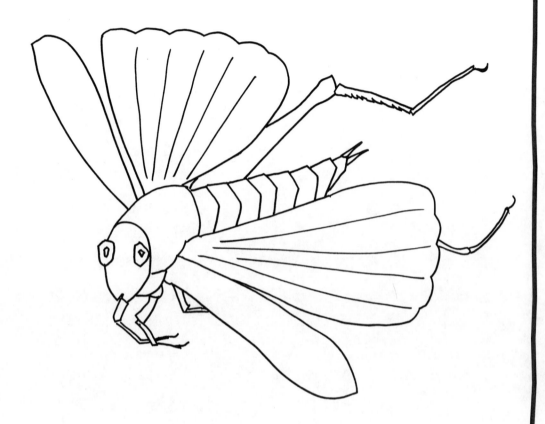

Try to make a picture of a very hungry caterpillar as he is about to eat each tasty treat.

Can you draw and color
a red barn under the bright sun?

A very quiet cricket is sneaking up on someone.
Can you draw a picture of who you think it is?

How would you decorate
this piece of tasty cake?

Seal begins with the letter *S*.
What other animals begin with *S*?
Can you draw one of them?

SEAL

Can you make a drawing of yourself camping in a tent? Hopefully these pesky mosquitoes don't bite!

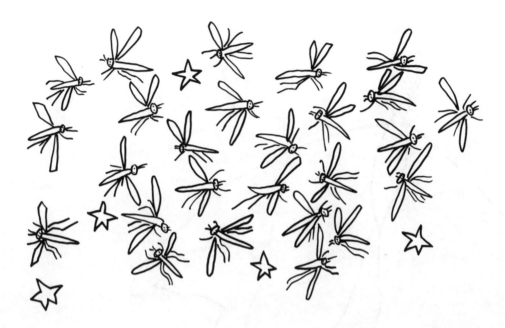

Can you decorate
the wings for this luna moth?

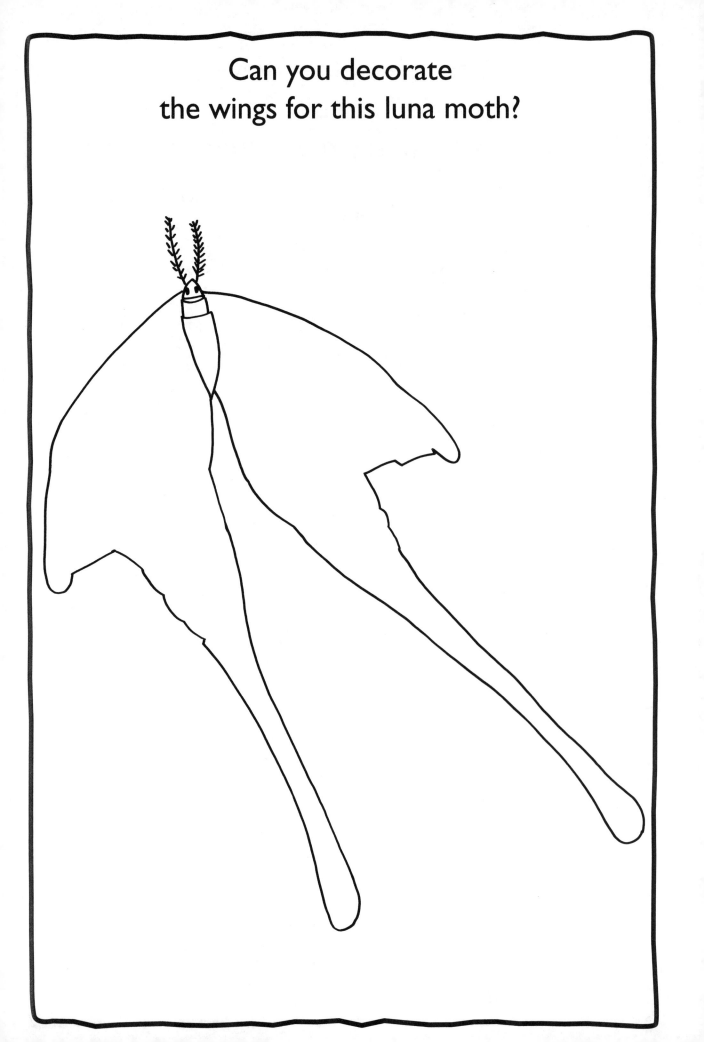

This cat has two colorful friends.
Can you make a drawing
of an orange cat and a yellow cat?

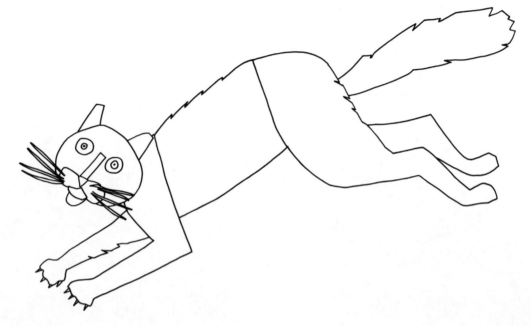

Doodlebug! Doodlebug!

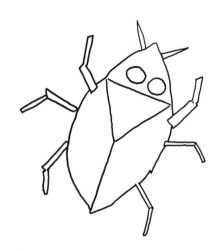

You might like to draw more apples on
this tree and some children under it!

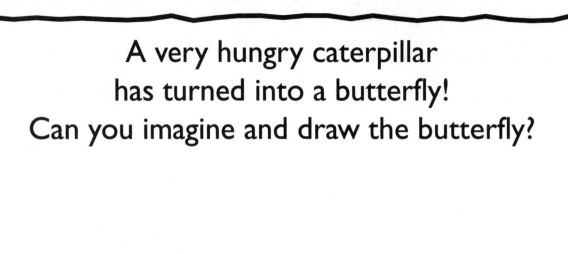

A very hungry caterpillar
has turned into a butterfly!
Can you imagine and draw the butterfly?

A flamingo is pink.
Can you draw and color
something else that is pink?

Can you draw and color a pond full of fish?

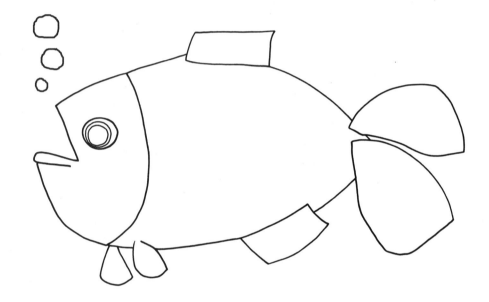

Try to draw a plate and a fork
for this piece of chocolate cake.
You might like to add a cherry on top, too!

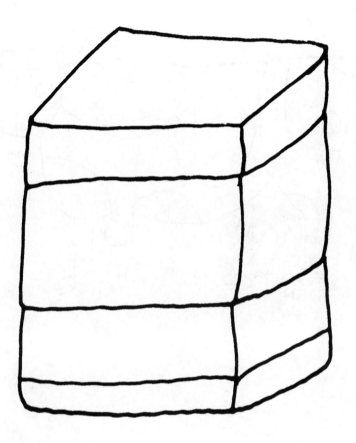

The cow is grazing in a green pasture.
Can you draw the pasture?
Where do the flowers and trees grow?

Where is the owl flying?
Can you draw what it is flying over?

This caterpillar is very full.
Can you draw a place for him to rest?

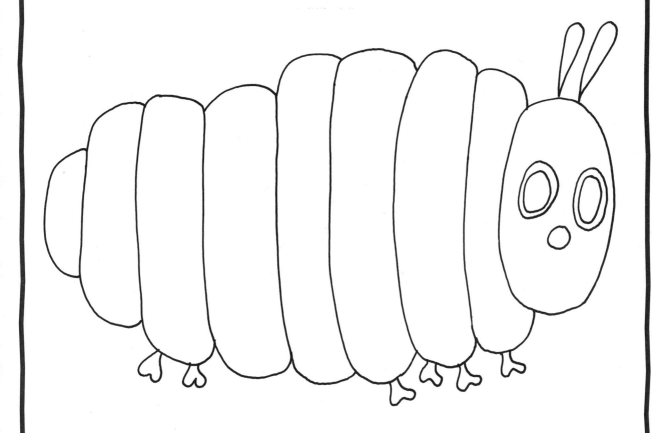

The sun is shining on your house.
Can you make a picture
of you and your friends playing?

Can you draw a rocky hill
for this mountain goat to climb?

Moo! The cow is ready to be milked.
Can you draw a picture of a milking pail
and a milking stool under the cow?

Can you draw a tree for the flying squirrel to land on?

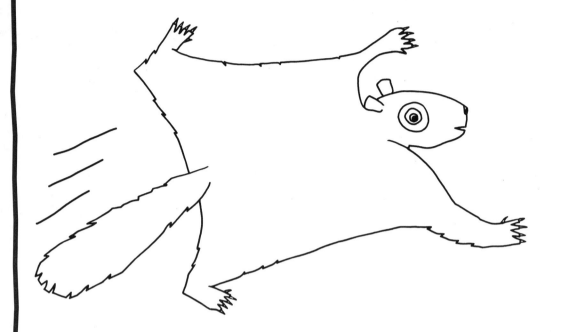

How many snakes are in the train car? Try to draw the same number of your favorite animal.

What does the grasshopper see?
Can you draw a picture of it?

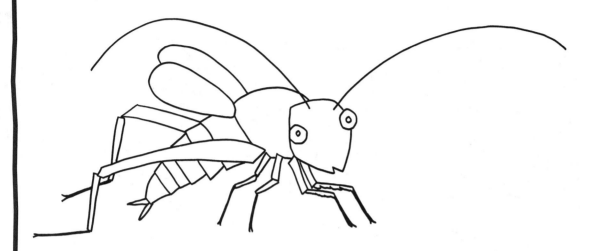

A very hungry caterpillar ate
through one piece of cherry pie.
Can you draw your favorite kind of pie?

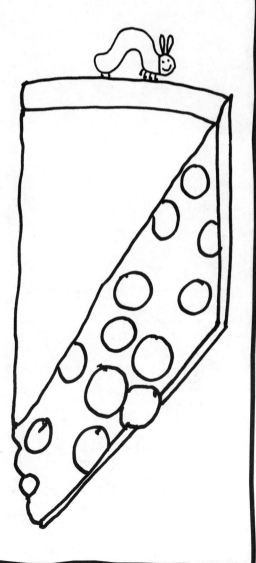

Can you make a picture of
some animals in a barnyard?

What is the gorilla looking at?
Can you draw it?

Can you finish the firefly
by drawing four wings on him?

What kind of tail can you draw for this cat?
Is it fluffy or thin?

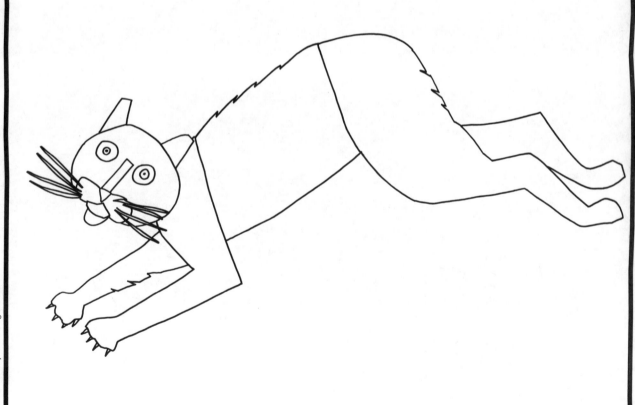

Doodlebug! Doodlebug!

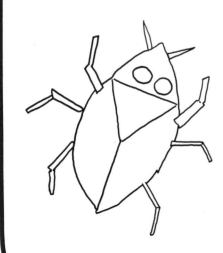

Can you draw a very hungry caterpillar eating this leaf?

Is this lonely firefly sad?
Can you draw a sad face?

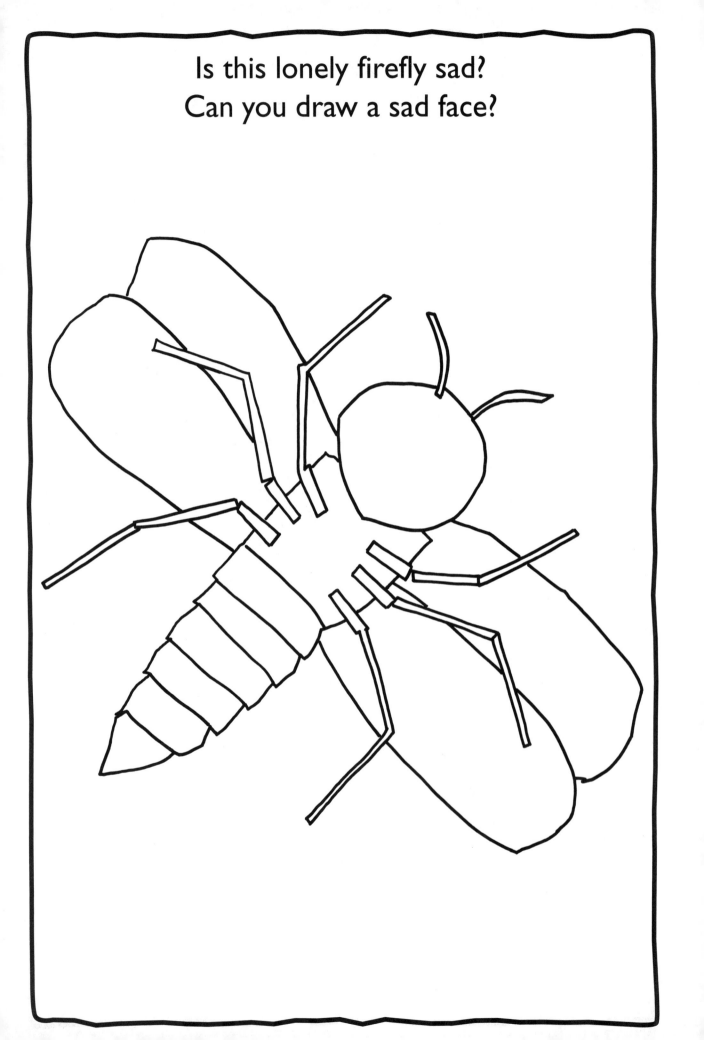

The lonely firefly meets a new friend!
Can you draw his new friend
and a happy face on the firefly?

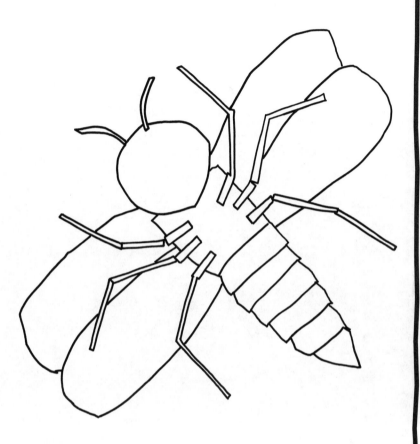

You might like to make a picture
of yourself with a happy face!

What are your three favorite ice cream flavors? Can you draw them in these cones?

You might like to decorate and
color the butterfly and his friend.

A buffalo is brown.
Is there another brown animal that you would like to draw?

Can you draw your favorite
crackers to go with this snack?

Can you draw a flock
of sheep for this dog to herd?

This boy is going to school.
What do you think his school looks like?

A very hungry caterpillar loves to eat fruit.
Can you draw him eating one
of the four strawberries?

A praying mantis has red eyes.
Try to dream up and draw
your own insect with red eyes!

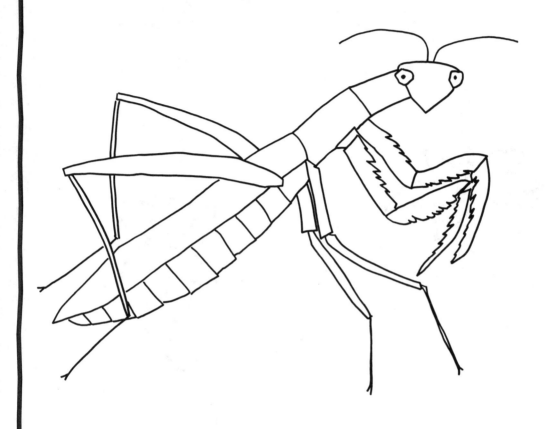

The elephant is eating from a pile of hay.
What does the hay look like?
Can you make a picture of hay?

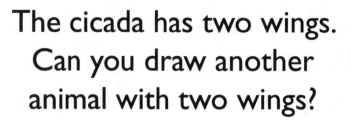

The cicada has two wings.
Can you draw another
animal with two wings?

A very hungry caterpillar wants to eat.
Can you draw another pear
and make it your favorite color?

A very busy spider is spinning her web.
Can you help her finish her work?

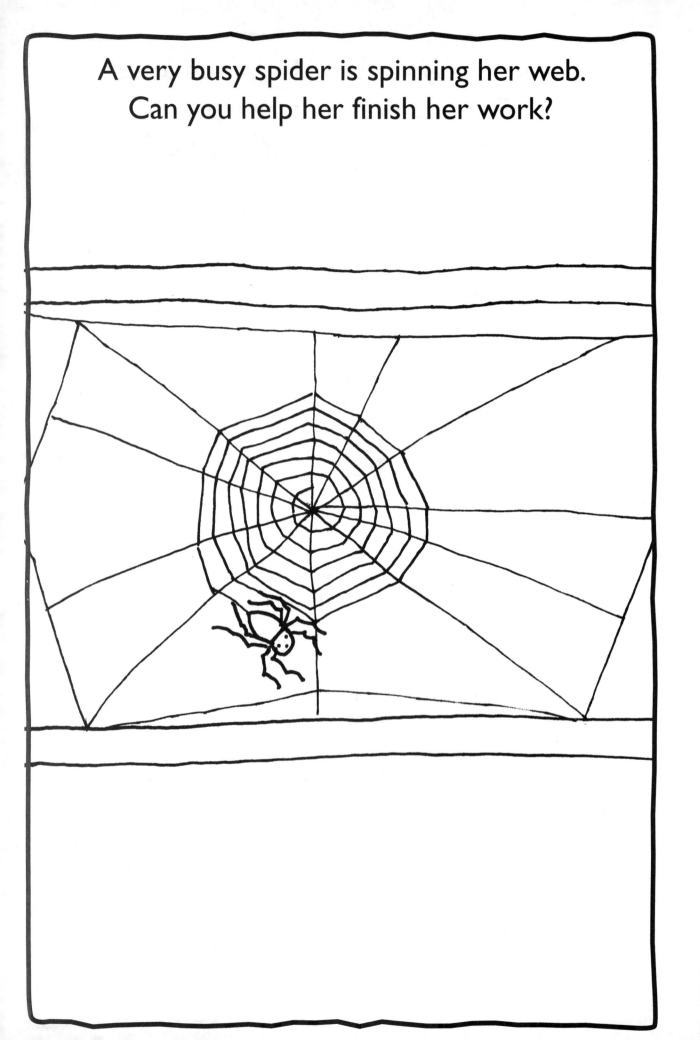

Oranges are orange.
What else would you like
to draw that is orange?

Can you draw a family
of swimming sea horses?

Doodlebug! Doodlebug!

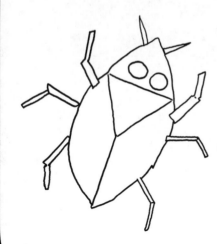

The bear is going for a walk.
Can you draw a path
for the bear to walk along?

Can you draw the insects that complete the patterns?

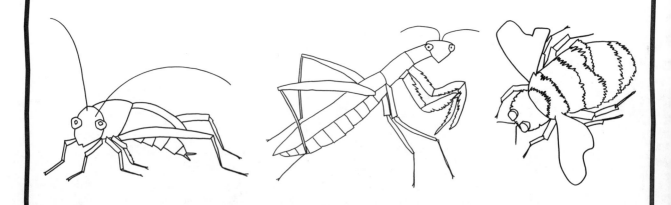

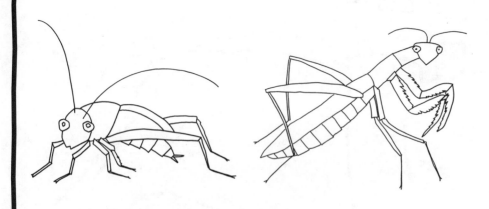

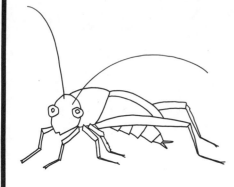

This bear has found the perfect place to nap.
Is it in the forest or in a cave?

Can you color the leaf green and then draw something else that is green?

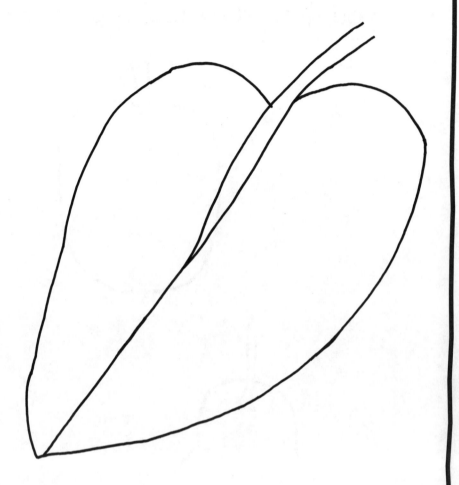

A very hungry caterpillar is going to eat
one apple, two pears, and three plums.
Can you draw the missing pear and two plums?

Try to make a picture of the food you like best!

The horse wants a drink of water.
Can you draw a trough and a water pump?

A very quiet cricket meets a spider.
Can you draw your own big, hairy spider?

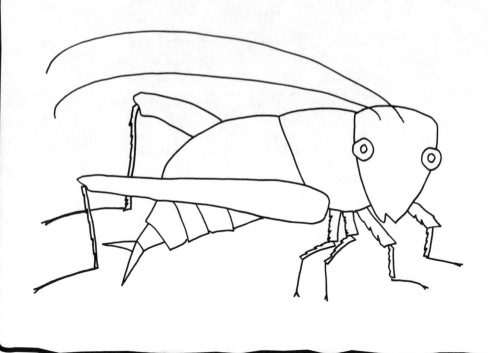

The pig is hungry.
Can you draw something for the pig to eat?

Can you draw an underwater scene?

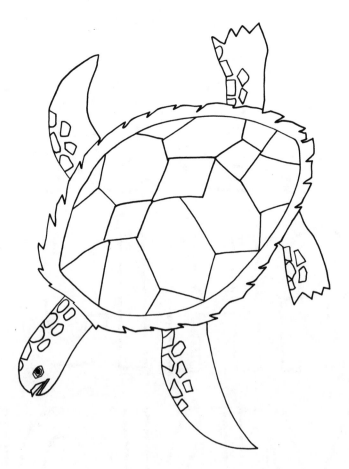

Can you color the letters
in a friend's name?

ABCDEF
GHIJKL
MNOPQ
RSTUV
WXYZ

The sun is going down.
You might like to draw some clouds
and add the colors of the sunset.

What is this cat growling at?

Can you think of and draw an insect for the praying mantis to hunt?

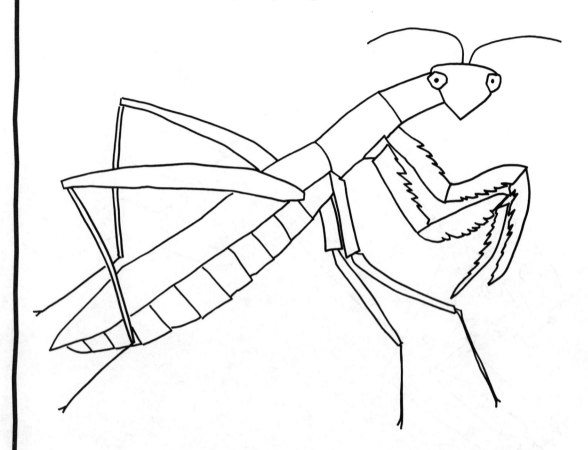

The cat wants her supper.
Can you draw a bowl of milk?

A heron has two wings.
Is there another creature with
two wings that you can draw and color?

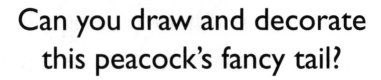
Can you draw and decorate
this peacock's fancy tail?

A bumblebee has yellow and black stripes.
Can you imagine and draw your
own amazing animal with stripes?

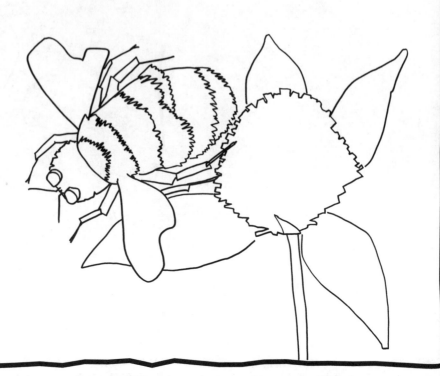

Can you draw yourself ready
to go on a fantastic adventure?
The parrot waves goodbye!

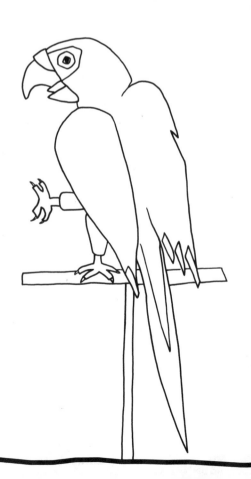